About the Author

Writing has always been an expression of thought and feeling to me. There is no better pleasure than putting the pen to paper and letting it morph into something I could be proud of. In the years since I was born and raised in Barbados, my eyes have been opened to many aspects of life. My passion started as a simple hobby, from little story ideas in school evolving into outlined plots I wanted to execute. It is a dream of mine not only to touch my audience with this and future works, but to evoke a deeper level of thought.

Wonders of the Dark

Klarin Dane

Wonders of the Dark

Olympia Publishers
London

www.olympiapublishers.com
OLYMPIA PAPERBACK EDITION

Copyright © Klarin Dane 2021

The right of Klarin Dane to be identified as author of
this work has been asserted in accordance with sections 77 and 78
of the Copyright, Designs and Patents Act 1988.

All Rights Reserved

No reproduction, copy or transmission of this publication
may be made without written permission.
No paragraph of this publication may be reproduced,
copied or transmitted save with the written permission of the
publisher, or in accordance with the provisions
of the Copyright Act 1956 (as amended).

Any person who commits any unauthorised act in relation to
this publication may be liable to criminal
prosecution and civil claims for damage.

A CIP catalogue record for this title is
available from the British Library.

ISBN: 978-1-78830-985-1

This is a work of fiction.
Names, characters, places and incidents originate from the writer's
imagination. Any resemblance to actual persons, living or dead, is
purely coincidental.

First Published in 2021

Olympia Publishers
Tallis House
2 Tallis Street
London
EC4Y 0AB

Printed in Great Britain

Acknowledgements

First and foremost, I thank God for guiding me to where I am today. There are many times when I've doubted my own ability, but I have to dutifully thank my support system for sticking with me through it all.

Samara, my biggest gas provider (she gets it), I'm so glad I've had you at my side pushing me towards greater things in life. You mean so much to me and I wouldn't trade our time together for anything. Faith, most definitely my biggest fan and scrutiniser. I appreciate you beyond words. You've helped allay any doubts I've had and helped me to see things clearly. Jason, Tyrell and Josh; my longest friendships. You've all seen me at my highest and my lowest, always believing that I could be great and pushed me to be so much better than just that. I couldn't have asked for more. You've read and given advice on anything I wrote, even helping me scout and push to find opportunity. Treshonia; I've nothing short of love for you. Such a kind and gentle soul who believed in my work, helping to keep me grounded in any venture I undertook. I thank you.

To the Gaffers United (you know who you are), you may

not know it, but you guys spurred me on to better myself and pursue new avenues. Seeing us all grow and move forward in life has helped to keep my head straight, and I couldn't have asked for a more solid friend group. Our time since Queen's College till now has been treasured. To Shanna and Kris, I'm glad to have you both on my team. You've given me a kick when needed and also been very supportive of my passion when others weren't.

Brandon. What can I say, you have believed in my writing so much so that you've ventured to work with me in future. I'm forever grateful to you and your faith in me as a writer and I hope to live up to that standard. Samantha and Dylana; to have family support me is a blessing, and I thank you for giving me support throughout my journey. Rontee: my fellow writer and someone dear to my heart. You've been at my side trying to help me grow as a writer and have always made sure I was aware of existing opportunities. I wish nothing but success for you in your career and I'll support you every step of the way. I appreciate you and your belief in me despite my style and preference not being your own.

To my current and future readers, I'm ecstatic to have you on board with me during this journey. None of this would be possible without you, and your support means the world to me. I will be sure to provide you with quality work both now and in future. Thank you.

Finally, to Olympia Publishers and staff, I am grateful that you have taken a chance on a budding author such as I with no name. Your interest in my work and my talent is greatly appreciated, and I thank you for the opportunity to dip my foot in the vast ocean that is writing. I look forward to many good years together in partnership, so let me just say... thank you.

Shattered

Murky skies cast dim shadows over a lonely street; small droplets of its tears badgering ephemeral life as though mourning the eventual loss of their time. The cover of darkness fast approached, like gloomy tendrils swallowing the light intent on catching young Lahir where he lay. His body was motionless, and a pair of crestfallen green eyes gazed upon the sky hoping to garner a sense of peace. He was dying. The crimson ichor humans needed to survive oozed from a gaping laceration spanning his torso, and with it, his consciousness.

Do you want to live?

The sweet, melodic sound of a woman's voice graced Lahir's ear… or was it his mind? He couldn't tell. Blurred vision obscured his surroundings, offering him no reprieve. He couldn't muster the energy to move his lips, yet he so strongly wanted to speak. He hadn't any intentions on meeting death today yet mangled on the street he lay, the life fading quickly from his weakened body. The tears came as his frustration mounted. His voice wouldn't aid him although his heart screamed yes. As the last of his consciousness faded, he heard her voice once more.

Fear not my child. I have heard your cries.

Cool air gently kissed Lahir's cheek, rousing him to greet a new day. Deep-blue curtains blew softly in the wind to the side of his room, obscuring some of the sun's rays. His body felt more relaxed than it'd ever been, resting on a delicate feather bed. Lahir sat upright and checked his body, noticing a large scar where his wound had previously been, but it had healed entirely. He vaguely remembered a voice offering to save him and moved to find and thank his saviour.

The room he'd been placed in was exquisite, its wooden walls and floors coated with a lustrous lavender lacquer, the area decorated with unique elegant ornaments sitting atop smooth varnished oak dressers. Their shapes were absurd, as though some otherworldly existence had handcrafted each with meticulous attention to detail. It was peaceful. His body felt better than ever before, and his surroundings were of such a tranquil nature he'd not even thought about what happened to him.

Lahir got off the bed and exited his room into a short hallway which opened up into a lounge below. A small group of individuals conversed there, laughing, teasing each other. They seemed to be close. Of the people there, two of the girls and one guy seemed to be his age whilst the other two were an aged man and young girl. Upon noticing him they'd beckoned him to come, apparently welcoming him to their home.

Despite feeling at ease, Lahir remained tethered to his position. He didn't know any of these people nor would he blindly trust any of them. His refusal to move garnered him looks of intrigue, and it surprised him to see that no one was offended. The aged man leisurely rose from his seat, manoeuvring through the lounge to make his way up the stairs toward Lahir. Upon the old man's arrival at the stair bottom, a wintry feeling of dread washed over Lahir. His hair stood on end, his palms sweating profusely.

"D-d-don't come any closer," Lahir stuttered.

Fear had gotten the better of him. Why'd the air change the closer that old man got? What is he? An array of questions cascaded in his mind, none of which he thought he wanted the answer to. Lahir took a half step back, planting his foot on something soft. There wasn't anything on the floor when he first came down the hallway, and he was too afraid to look behind him now.

"I'd appreciate it if you removed your foot."

Someone was behind him? He hadn't heard so much as a footstep or been aware of a presence so close to him until they were actually there. The cold, harsh tone in their voice was hard to miss, as if they already hated him. Dangerous. His body had said as much, yet he was glued to his spot, unable to muster the courage to run. A gentle touch to his back sent chills down his spine, and the frosty tips of fingers caused Lahir to jerk forward.

Slowly turning to see the aggressor, Lahir was awestruck. The energy he'd felt from being in close proximity to her directly contrasted with her outward appearance. She was gorgeous… unlike any woman he'd ever seen. Soft, despondent green eyes peered into him, and her shoulder length curly light brown hair accentuated her caramel skin. She had two books in her hand and sighed as she moved past Lahir.

"You should evaluate how you treat those trying to help you."

Her tone made it clear that she thought little of Lahir, yet it hadn't seemed as though he was the sole recipient of her ill-mannered ways. She brushed past the older man, ignoring both him and those in the lounge to occupy a solitary spot just out of earshot in order to read. His nerves had settled, and the old man made his way up the stairs and gave him a reassuring pat on the back.

"I apologise on behalf of Aaliyah," he said, "she can be quite intense. Pay it no heed. I'm Grant by the way. What's your name?"

"...It's Lahir."

The feeling of terror, those dreadful waves he'd felt earlier, had vanished as Aaliyah left his presence. Grant's voice became a distant echo as Lahir's thoughts drowned any sound that may reach him. Clouded, his mind tried to make sense of his new surroundings, and what that girl's existence here might mean for him. He was worried. Should he leave? He clutched his chest, experiencing genuine unease at the thought of going through what he did before he woke here.

Grant snapped his fingers, beckoning Lahir back to reality. His gaze seemed to be one of genuine worry, and Lahir noticed that the youngest of the group had joined the old man, clinging to his leg. He'd zoned out for an extensive period, unaware of his environment.

"If you need some time to rest and take it all in that's fine," Grant began, "we'll be downstairs when you're ready."

Grant placed a reassuring hand on Lahir's shoulder, slightly easing his discomfort. Noticing the child's unease, Lahir, convinced he was the cause, managed a faint smile.

"I'm sorry," he said bending to meet the child's eyes, "I was a bit shaken. What do you do for fun around here?"

The girl's eyes lit up, excited to engage in fun activities and tear away from simple conversation amongst the older individuals. She'd motioned to Grant that she wanted to go outside, but Grant held her close, gesturing for her to wait.

Lahir followed Grant and the young girl to the others in the lounge, where they all drank and exchanged names and light-hearted stories. As the afternoon continued, the group ventured outside, giving Lahir a tour of the cabin and its surroundings.

The cabin was deep in the woods, almost entirely encircled by healthy trees. The distant canopy above left minor openings, allowing rays of sunlight to cast an orange tinge beneath their shade. The sound of the leaves swaying in the breeze was calming, and a rugged stone path that seemed as if it had seen some years through the weather and other elements marked the way through and out of the forest.

"Lahir!" Alice squealed with excitement. The young girl's happy-go-lucky personality had come out in full effect following their chat in the lounge and had persisted since. "Let's go down to the lake! To the lake!"

Clara, the darker toned of the two older girls, had placed her hand on Alice's head, asking her to be patient. Her dark eyes held an intensity that made it difficult to avert her gaze. Despite her being one of the youngest present, Lahir noticed that she was the bedrock of the group. She was pretty; her silky black hair tied up in a bun suited her well, though her regal demeanour far outshone any of her other traits.

The group had decided to make their way toward the lake despite the setting sun, much to Lahir's dismay. He wasn't fond of the idea of being outside at night in strange woods and he made that clear to the group. Following a solid pat on the back from what had to be the most muscular person Lahir had ever seen, he'd let out a cough and stumbled forward.

"Wh-what was that about Tevin?" Lahir choked.

Tevin let out a friendly bellow before placing his hand on Lahir's shoulder. His gaze shifted soon after and became serious.

"Listen…" he began. His tone was firm, solemn. "We've all been saved from death. I'm sure you heard a voice calling to you once you were fading. We were all saved by an angel, and this area is her domain. As long as we don't cross the bridge leading off this isle, no harm can befall us."

"What bridge?"

"It's about a mile's walk out from the lake, but none of us have ever left."

"Haven't you thought of going back to your life? Your family—"

Denise interrupted the conversation, questioning Lahir's thoughts.

"What exactly would we be going back to?"

The girl's long white hair flowed down to her lower back, and her soft blue eyes held his gaze.

"Our lives. There's more to the world than being boxed in."

"None of us have led easy lives, and we all technically met awful ends. If we leave… we will someday meet a similar end. That's what the angel told us."

"A caged life of fear is no better than being dead."

Lahir's tone aggravated Denise, and their conversation became a heated back-and-forth disagreement, leading up to the group deciding to take Lahir to the angel. They made their way through the forest sticking to the path until they came upon diverging pathways. Lahir knew the right was towards the lake, but the group veered left.

The dusk of night quickly approached, and the cobblestones were illuminated by the majesty of a crescent moon. It'd been about ten minutes before they reached a marble altar. Accented by an assortment of flowers and lush shrubbery, two pillars mirroring the forest around them rose from the ground, adorning the shrine with nature's beauty.

Clara made her way forward and placed a wooden totem on the altar. Soon after, the skies had been parted with a radiant, glistening light. The angel was everything he'd expected one to be. Pure, white wings graced the night with all their majesty as she descended to meet the humans she'd saved. Her golden hair fell to her shoulders, smooth as silk and her starry eyes set their focus on Lahir. She wore a simple toga, and not a single jewel could be found on her body. She just felt… godly.

Lahir found himself bowing without being aware, thanking her for helping him and giving him a second chance at life. The angel spoke her name: Lucaiel, and she held Lahir in her embrace before having a long conversation with him and subsequently the group. Her aura reminded him of a mother's love. It was safe. Lahir wanted to stay with her, and after hearing her reiterate Denise's tale of going back to the outside world, he decided to take some time to himself under her protection on the isle.

Collectively, with Lucaiel following close behind, the group made their way to the lake. The reality that he'd someday meet his end in the same fashion as before if he chose to leave weighed on Lahir's mind. Despite the revelation, he'd wanted to return to his life, his family, friends. He was grateful to Lucaiel for saving him and felt forever indebted, but he would someday have to say goodbye to her.

- The lake was a massive body of water with the silver shimmer of moonlight rippling on its surface. Alice ran off down the jetty and jumped in, unable to contain her excitement. The others chuckled and followed suit, enjoying a late-night swim at the foot of an illustrious mountain. No one had ever been able to approach this isle to see it up close, thwarted by a seemingly invisible barrier, making them only able to gaze from afar. Curiosity often brought tourists to the location, and the unexplained reason behind humans' inability to breach the island was now clear to him.

Lahir remained on land, smiling as he watched them play.

"Do you not want to join?" Lucaiel asked.

"I'll go soon. It's just a lot to take in but I think I could get used to this."

Lucaiel sat, paying close attention to Lahir, intrigued by how many gears turned in his head constantly. She knew he wasn't entirely at ease and beckoned him toward her. He was allowed to rest on her lap, and she cradled him.

"Care to tell me what's on your mind?"

"It's Aaliyah. She doesn't seem to be a part of this unit… frankly, she scares me. Something feels off about her."

"Aaliyah is difficult. She has a great distaste for humans because of her past and though she prefers solitude, she's actually a very kind-hearted individual. In time she may come around."

Since he had been with his saviour, time was fleeting. The night raced on, and the group had made their way back to the cabin to rest. Lucaiel stayed overnight, watching over her 'children' and ascending at daybreak. She'd recast a blessing on the entire isle, ensuring their safety and peace of mind.

The days following Lahir's first had been easy, filled with happy moments and new memories. He'd became close with the people there save Aaliyah, who still made him uneasy every time she was around.

Although only a short time had passed, he felt as though these few months had created an unbreakable bond between them, but now, it was time to go.

Everyone gathered to bid their farewells in a melancholic mood, each wanting him to stay. Aaliyah had, surprisingly, taken some time from her books to see him off, and Lahir was happy she'd come; even if he'd thought she was weird.

"Death is a luxury you won't experience."

Typical. She hadn't been nice to him during his stay; what reason would she have to be now? Lahir's discomfort with her statement was plastered on his face and she seemed satisfied with playful smile across her face.

"It's a line from a book I read," she chuckled, "I thought it might be fun to see your reaction."

Lahir had now seen it all. What was more puzzling? Was it that she'd attempted a joke and he was there to witness or was it the revelation that she might actually like him? His mood was lighter, and he ventured across the bridge off the isle… back into society.

The first few weeks had been great. He managed to find work, rekindle his relationships with old friends and family and had even found a decent place to stay. He'd felt blessed. His proximity to Lucaiel for an extended time had done wonders for him and he'd decided he would live his life to the best of his ability.

As time passed, Lahir had received a promotion, and decided to celebrate the night with friends and go out for drinks. With the passing of the night, Lahir's head got lighter and he felt giddy. He was enjoying his time and was disappointed it had to end; bidding farewell to his friends as they parted ways. The walk home would take a while since he stumbled, pausing every few steps.

The streets were bustling with people enjoying the nightlife and Lahir bumped into a few of them, trying to navigate his way out of the gap. He thought he might've been imagining things, as he'd seen a man who resembled himself propped against a pole, blood trickling down his face from two empty eye sockets. Lahir rubbed his eyes, and the disturbing image was gone. He was hallucinating. He'd had too much to drink.

After a long walk returning home, he'd made his way inside running to hug the toilet as the vomit built up in his throat. He felt awful. His mouth blazed as though he'd somehow acquired the throat of a fire-breathing dragon. Time felt slowed, as if the feeling would remain with him indefinitely. An eerie croon echoed in his mind, and he felt the sensation of cold fingertips trace the length of his back. Turning slightly to his side, his blurred vision outlined a woman's figure, much to his shock.

"Hi," Lahir managed.

The humming continued.

"Who are you?"

His vision cleared and his body tensed. The awful feeling he'd had was replaced with another. Terror. He was no longer in his room, instead he was faced with a discoloured, two-toned entity, riddled with an array of markings along her shadowy body and a dislocated jaw in a dark cube with no physical structure. He opened his mouth, but the sound wouldn't come out.

The humming stopped

Shaken and afraid that the thing in front of him would be the reason his life ended, Lahir quickly pulled a totem from his pocket. It was a gift from Lucaiel, and it cast a piercing light that repelled the spirit ahead of him and dispelled the space he'd been trapped in.

He was in his room once more, and he thought that maybe his death was nearing. The events that Lucaiel and the others had warned him about may soon come to pass, and without a thought, Lahir had run out and stole his neighbour's car. They had a tendency to leave their keys in the visor, a foolish oversight he was thankful for in the moment. He was going back to the isle. Death wasn't an option. Making it past the bridge was his priority, he'd be safe then.

After some time, Lahir had safely arrived, passing the bridge and heading directly to the cabin. He burst through the door only to find Aaliyah alone in the lounge, reading. He was relieved to see a familiar face and made his way towards her.

"Back so soon?" she asked.

Lahir hugged her against his better judgement and explained why he'd returned. She was sympathetic towards him, comforting and staying with him. He'd concluded that he'd never be able to understand Aaliyah, but he was grateful to her.

"The others are asleep for now."

Lahir expressed his thanks to Aaliyah, letting her know he intended to go see Lucaiel. He was no longer afraid now that he was within her domain and it hadn't taken long before he called the angel, and was face to face with her regality.

She held him close, aware of what he'd been through, showering him in a friendly radiant light. A black cloud was forced out of him from the area where he'd been touched and Lucaiel warned him about the danger he'd face if he left the island again.

Faced with the reality that he couldn't leave lest he be targeted by some demonic entity, Lahir felt caged in. Noticing his sullen mood, the angel allowed him to rest on her lap where he promptly fell asleep. He'd tackle his worries in the morning. He'd just need to adjust to having no contact outside of the isle. This was his happy ending.

Lahir woke to a sweet, soothing melody. Lucaiel was singing to him, and her voice was amazing. He opened his eyes to gaze upon the being he owed his life to, only to be greeted by two bottomless pits of darkness peering into his soul. Whatever held him shouldn't be here. Where was Lucaiel? Lahir was unable to move, held in place somehow, only able to soak in the malignant smile of a grey-faced spotted demon.

"Lu...cai...el."

The demon held the totem Lahir had received, and its form disappeared, driving fear deeper into Lahir's bones.

"Despair."

It was the voice he'd heard call to him that fateful night. This was the true face of the entity that had saved him.

"Is it born from simple fear?" it asked, gently stroking his hair, "or is it born from a shattered reality? What does the realisation that Lucaiel, the cabin, the people... the idea of living harmoniously under divine protection have all been an illusion make you feel?"

Lahir was dumbfounded. He was

speechless... helpless.

"I let you die that night. You are nothing but a soul on whom I have bestowed senses. Your life and experiences since that day have been a lie. The reason you were targeted by another demon is because, in reality, you were a wandering soul."

Lahir had a blank, broken expression on his face. The demon cradling him smiled and held him against her chest, satisfied with his shattering mind, and the two slowly seeped through a hazy swirl. A whisper of the last words Lahir would ever comprehend came next.

Your soul will be mine always.

Reflection

Droplets of water constantly kissed the cold concrete floor, slowly oozing from a rusted broken pipe above. Terian sat chained to the wall, boxed in by an alarming number of slowly fanning shutters filtering in small amounts of light. Shadows slowly scurried across the room running from the light with each cycle upward and down by the shutters.

When the shutters were up, the light slightly illuminated the face of yet another captive, not yet awake, and lying face first on the freezing floor. Terian felt a wave of hate and frustration wash over him; he wondered what wrong he could've done in his life to warrant being held captive in the same room as the person responsible for his life's upheaval, and he felt unable to do anything about his feelings.

The person was gagged, though aside from their inability to cohesively answer Terian's questions when they'd awoken, it was not an issue. Terian noticed the change in his hair's pigment since he'd been here. It was the graceful white of snow before it met the ground, induced by his perceived level of stress over time.

The passing of a few hours felt like days, as he sat succumbing to the reality of no escape. In this prison, time was torture, and before long, a day had passed; two. The growing stench emanating from a pile of Terian's waste was becoming naught but a mildly displeasing aroma. It had taken some time, but his roommate had finally opened their eyes.

"Ah..." Terian began, "you're awake."

His voice was calm, devoid of the rage he'd felt a couple days ago and instead he regarded his struggling and squirming cellmate with cold contempt. Despite their muffled cries for help and unsuccessful attempts at escape, Terian continued as though the other person were casually sitting in a chair unburdened by the confines of a dilapidated room.

"Do you remember who I am?" Terian asked flatly, "I suppose not."

Terian scratched his head, staring deeply into a pair of hazel eyes as though he were peering into their soul. The chains bound to his arms rattled as he sat up, moving into a pose for meditation.

"I sometimes wonder what makes us human. What defines who we are as people. Is there truly a right way to do things in this world? Or are we all wrong?"

Muffled cries and incomprehensible words from a frightened cellmate fell on Terian's ears and he nodded as if he understood everything.

"The average person sees it all in black and white. Did you know that?" Terian's voice became lower and colder. "Right or wrong. Every action we take falls into one of these categories based upon our beliefs, but there is one thing I've always wondered. Why do we always identify truly despicable acts as those involving children?"

Terian's meditation pose faltered, and he once more

looked at the bound cell mate, whose eyes widened upon the light shining on Terian's face again. They'd finally recognised him, struggling with intense determination to escape now.

"You know..." Terian chuckled while covering one eye, staring intensely through the other at his companion, "if you take my child from me as an adult... is it any different from me taking yours as a toddler? We love our children unconditionally. It's no different at birth than when they're fully grown adults. Parental instinct? Who knows?"

Terian smiled. It was sadistic and haunting; it made his companion in solitude retreat to a corner, terrified.

"My family was taken from me," he chuckled, "law enforcement failed me and yet they siphon all that I have left to live. Is this justice? To suffer at the hands of those who've wronged you with no reprieve? Yet... if I take your child from you... would I face... justice? I truly detest the concept. All those who claim to fight for it veer drastically from its true meaning. I do not seek justice. I seek nothing but to murder you. Slowly. Painfully. I will revel in your screams... bathe in your blood and destroy what you hold dear. Sadly... these chains shackle me from fulfilling my desire."

Fear became apparent in Terian's companion's antics as they wrestled with the chains attempting escape, and Terian revelled in their discomfort and frantic struggle.

"I don't think you understand me very well. We all wear faces. The world sees the face we show them... but is it possible to change the way they perceive what they see? Children are seen as innocent..."

Terian paused. His smile was unnerving.

"What if I were to wear the face of your child? Would I then be seen as innocent? Would I then receive the 'justice' that is owed to me?"

Terian's enemy violently tugged on his chains in an attempt to get close to him, enraged at Terian's threatening comment about his child. Thoughts of murder, sadness and a bright future echoed incessantly within Terian's mind, drowning the noises made by his companion and he let out a nervous laugh.

"Ah the rage…" Terian said as he eased forward, "But do you have ANY right to be! YOUR ANGER… HOW CAN YOU FEEL IT WHEN YOU'VE TAKEN MY CHILD FROM ME! DO YOU DESERVE TO HAVE SOMETHING TO LIVE FOR?"

Terian's voice broke, devolving into a solemn cry. He sounded weary, as though he'd long reached his limit.

"Taking from you what you took from me doesn't make me evil. It doesn't make me good. I've come to a plane of existence where my actions have no meaning. Can you comprehend it? It's said that children are fully imprinted by the time they're about seven. That means we can predict the type of human being they will be once they reach that age. Since my actions fall into a place with no meaning… it is neither right nor wrong for me to take the lives of the unenlightened, is it?"

The person opposite Terian had been brought to tears, with traces of snot oozing from their nose like jam from a doughnut after it was bitten.

"Yes… feel the despair," Terian whispered across the room, "this world needs to be cleansed. The innocent must survive while the evil ones die. As one who lies between the concepts of good and evil… I will administer judgement upon the unenlightened. To ensure this world does not reject me, I will wear the face of innocence. That leads to true justice."

The chains broke. Terian's smile widened, and he grew quiet. Taking in his surroundings once more, he noticed the disappearance of his companion. Instead, a pair of skeletons lay on the cold concrete floor, vaguely illuminated by the passing light. One was that of an adult, and the other a child. Terian gazed upon a fractured mirror, looking at his marred reflection with heightened interest. His face was no longer there. Instead, what stared back at him was the stretched face of a young girl no older than ten, stitched onto what once was his.

There was no trace left of his own identity; just layers of tissue and bone hidden behind the face of a child. Terian ran his fingers across the strained skin with smug satisfaction.

"This is true innocence."

A Broken Choice

Gentle waves caressed Selena's static body, washing away the not yet dried stains of blood covering her frame. She'd been gazing upon the starry night, completely lost in her thoughts.

The blood wasn't hers, but broken limbs prevented her pursuit of the one she tried to save: her son. How could her only child be taken away? She'd failed her son; had failed as both a parent and guardian.

The assailant had left her helpless, with sufficient damage to her throat to prevent any cries for help. Tears streamed down her face as she wrestled with the hopelessness of her situation. She was likely to die here; until then, she would forever be tormented by the image of her attacker dragging her battered son out to sea.

The pain was unbearable, and her vision blurred as her consciousness began to fade. Her thoughts were the only companions she had left; a simple prayer all she could offer.

If there is a God... please keep my son safe. Let him be the one to stay alive.

Darkness. It's all that was left after her consciousness faded along with her accepted fate.

***

A plain, blindingly white room cradled Selena as she rose

from her slumber, but as her eyes adjusted, she noticed her son playing with toy aeroplanes in one corner of the room. Once he'd realised she was awake, he immediately perked up and happily ran over to her, throwing himself over her lap.

"Mommy, Mommy!" he shouted cheerfully, "come fly the plane with me!"

Selena smiled as tiny droplets of water trickled down her face. Words couldn't express how she felt inside. Her son was here. He'd been left with scars across his body, but he was here. She could hold him, see him... a myriad of emotions overwhelmed her, and she hugged him tightly while nodding to him.

The damage to her throat had been permanent, leaving her without a voice. This seemed insignificant, though, now that she'd seen her son. She held his hand, following him to the corner and began to play with him. He was happy. She was happy. There had been a God after all. Now, she just needed time to recuperate before trying to leave this strange place. It might've been a medical facility, but she was unsure and hadn't heard or seen anyone else as yet.

As the day passed on, the pangs of hunger plagued both Selena and her son, prompting her to walk toward the door and call for someone. It was unlocked, which meant they weren't imprisoned. A faint smile graced her lips, though ephemeral in nature once the door had reached full swing.

Standing in the doorway was an uncanny mirror of herself, only... twisted. Her finger tips were dripping with blood, and her palms tightly gripped the blade of a knife. Unkempt hair covered a portion of her face, showing just enough to reveal bloodshot eyes that seemed so full of hate.

More unnerving than the wretched sight of herself peering within her very being was the bleak darkness behind it. The door hadn't led anywhere. She was in an isolated room, trapped with the son she refused to lose again and quickly slammed the door out of fear. Selena ran towards her son, cradling him in her arms as she tried to figure out how they could escape such a dire situation.

"Mommy who was that?"

"I don't know sweetie," she said trying to sound brave, "we'll go get something to eat now." Her voice had returned, slipping her notice as a result of her current internal panic.

She rubbed her son's back in an attempt to keep him calm while trying to hide her desperation. Aside from the door she'd tried to exit through, there was no other way to leave. She was completely barred off.

"Why do you flee?"

There was no sound indicating the door was opened, yet there it was, that person who closely resembled herself peering back at her as Selena looked over her shoulder. It was a terrifying sight, and Selena wondered why all of this was happening to her. She needed to find a way out with her son.

"Freedom always has a cost Selena… and I won't hinder that choice."

What does this… myself mean?

It seemed as though this person wouldn't stop her from leaving, and so Selena cautiously skirted around the imposter, clutching her uneasy son close to her chest. The constant stares from the fake person sent chills down the spine of Selena and her son, but she made her way to the door without incident and opened it.

There was an exit now which confused Selena, but she had to make a choice. Would she stay here in a room with a bloodied and dangerous person who had the same face as her? Or would she leave and take her son to safety through the hallway of the hospital she was in?

It wasn't a hard decision. Her son was her number one priority, and so she exited through the door, hoping never to see that imposter again. Selena hadn't encountered anyone while traversing the hall and she hadn't realised what it meant to experience something truly haunting until she walked through the hospital doors.

"Mommy... why did you leave me?"

Selena looked down at her son, horrified to the core by what she saw. His body was ripped to pieces, each of the previous scars outlining pieces of his corpse. Worse than that, the voice kept coming from her son's mangled body, as if it were some sick dream she was dragged into.

"I needed you... but you left me...why?"

It tore at her. The things she heard in her son's voice as the corpse seemingly vanished ripped her apart mentally. The scenery changed, and there she was, a confused mind in the middle of a bustling street walking towards a church.

Her son was gone, and these people laughed... enjoying their day as if to make a mockery of her. She felt like an outcast; a melancholic spirit waltzing amongst the living, falling deeper into the abyss the closer she got to the church.

"Would you care to serve our amazing God?"

The random lady on the corner of the street stopped Selena, provoking an eerie chuckle.

Amazing. The one who ignored my pleas... and let my son die... amazing? Ah... it must be a cruel joke. Fine.

Selena tightly gripped a jagged knife in her hand, unaware of where she'd acquired it. That wasn't important. What mattered was the pain this woman felt for suggesting what she did, and so Selena forcibly carved an innocent's body from a deep, initial puncture. That she bled profusely was of no consequence. Her screams were of no consequence. The one she called amazing would not save her... just as they hadn't saved her son.

As the life faded from her victim's eyes, her surroundings changed. She was now in the solitary wing of a prison, dressed as a guard and watching over a lone inmate. There was a jarring noise that kept pestering her, as if the inmate had been scraping against the door from the inside.

"So you're finally here."

Selena turned to face her imposter once more. Why was she here now?

"Have your choices been worth it?"

The scraping got louder.

"You ran from me. You desired freedom. And what did it cost? Your happiness. Running only led you back to me... do you know why?"

Selena felt torn, trembling and tearing up as she thought about it all. Was she the reason her son died? Whatever this person was... they had tried to warn her not to leave the room. Maybe if she'd stayed, she'd have kept her son... her happiness.

"I see you offer no answer. Maybe this will garner a response. When you lose your happiness... in search of freedom. What is there left to lose?"

"W-what do you mean?" Selena stammered.

"When all that's left is your anger. There is only one thing you have left to lose."

Selena felt a sharp pain course through her abdomen as trails of blood escaped her lips. The imposter held her close, smiling as she removed the shard of glass.

"Goodnight my dear."

These would be the last words she heard before her neck was snapped, allowing the fake one to assume her identity. It was cruel; a fate she did not deserve, yet it was the one she received.

***

A gagged man strapped to a chair desperately tried to escape, his muffled cries a minor annoyance falling on deaf ears. The imposter who'd murdered Selena sat calmly at the victim's feet, slowly peeling the skin off his toes while singing a song to herself.

As the sun sets
So the curtain falls
I wonder what we'll find behind these walls
A finger, a flower, our price is met
Now let's, enjoy, our time...
Or we'll be left behind
We write the final chapter...
And now your life is mine.

Lake Sym

The orange tinge of the setting sun painted an enthralling portrait of Lake Sym. It sat in a basin cradled by towering mountains and a thick surrounding fog. Days and nights here had always been lonely; calm. The water was undisturbed, and the silence made almost any noise appear deafening.

Wildlife was non-existent within a two-mile radius of the lake, as if they instinctively avoided the area. The eerie aura around the calm body of water sent icy chills down the spines of anyone who dared approach, deterring both locals and tourists alike.

Back in the small town Symeria, the usual silent alleys had seen a huge ruckus in the form of a teen boy. Law enforcement had been chasing him for quite some time; a walking plague terrorising their humble abodes. Several counts of theft had been traced back to him and there were suspicions of murder directed at him.

The boy was a crisis looming over the townsfolk; one they'd all been sure was responsible for all of their misgivings. He'd eluded them for years through an array of deceptive techniques and constantly being on the move. There was never any concrete trace left in areas he'd temporarily settled, but today they would not allow him to escape.

The officers chasing him had wounded him; the

blood from a bullet hole in his abdomen oozing out at a dangerous rate. The boy managed to shake them using his knowledge of back alleys and the terrain, but it was only a matter of time before they caught up to him using the bloodstained ground as a trail.

Hope for the scent of rain betrayed him, dampening his chances of escape even further. He couldn't make it back to his camp like this, and even if he did, the police would know exactly where he was thanks to his wound. There was no other choice left, and he hobbled towards the start of the path leading to the lake.

Rails made of rope outlined the safest walkway to the lake, and the boy made sure to firmly grip the rope, neither loosening his grip on it nor the pressure on his wound. As he painfully trudged down the walkway, his vision became obscured as a result of a thickening fog the further he moved. His body was beginning to give out and he collapsed barely halfway down the trail. He wouldn't be able to make it.

The blurred silhouette of a person was the last thing he'd seen as his consciousness faded. Had they caught up to him already? He couldn't afford to be caught, but his body was at its limit. He would be executed for murders he hadn't committed, and he wasn't ready to die.

***

Lunar rays pierced through the dense fog, and the boy had awoken to find himself propped against the trunk of a tree. His wound had been tended to, and he couldn't make out where the path was. Someone had helped him…but who?

There were voices in the distance, which he soon recognised as those of his pursuers. The police were determined to capture him and despite being subject to first aid, his body was unable to handle any sudden or rapid movement. They'd never come so close to the lake before. Why now?

Risking their own lives by coming to the lake seemed extreme just to capture him, and he was sure there was something he'd been missing. He was being accused of something he had no idea about. It was the only explanation he could find to explain why they'd shot on sight and pursued him this far.

The sound of rustling leaves sent a shiver down his spine. Something was close, but he couldn't make out anything in the fog even with the help of illuminating moonbeams. He stayed quiet, taking special care not to reveal his position, positive that whatever it was would have trouble noticing him just as he found difficulty seeing through the fog.

He suddenly caught a whiff of a scent reminiscent of the ocean, and a sweet aroma one might find on a woman. Turning to his left, there it was. He still couldn't make out what it was, but those piercing green eyes had made him anxious. He was sweating bullets, and he'd fallen out of fear, reopening his wound.

Unintentionally, he let out a loud wail of pain, signalling his position to his pursuers, who had turned their attention to the cry's origin. He desperately clutched his wound, attempting to crawl away, avoiding both his pursuers and the pair of green eyes that kept staring at him.

"You shouldn't move around so much… or my help would've been for naught."

He paused. The voice was soothing; melodic. Turning back to the voice's origin, he noticed those green eyes once again and despite its sweetness, what he'd gotten was a look of contempt and distaste.

"Why were you here?"

In the dead silence of night, the footsteps of his pursuers grew ever closer. He had to get away. Forcing his body to move, he tried to stand and run but that too, like his escape, was now a dream. There was a light grip on his left leg for a brief moment, and in that instant, he'd heard a snap.

The still night had been broken by a deafening cry of anguish. The beams of flashlights wavered frantically just a short distance away now in the fog. They were close, but it seemed he was caught by something more dangerous than the police themselves and he urinated on himself as he was dragged onto the pier by the lake.

It was clear here, devoid of the obscuring tendrils of fog masking the lake's surroundings. He hadn't stopped wincing in pain as a result of his injuries but felt as though it was somehow a bad dream. His captor was a woman short of stature, with silky black hair decorated with seashells. She was completely naked, and had claw-like scars across her abdomen and cheek. Her gaze was intense, and he felt as though she would take his life before the police had a chance.

"I hate being ignored."

Her voice was cold, and the strength she displayed to

hoist him above her was ridiculous.

"I'll ask once more. Why were you here?"

"Hold it right there!"

The officers had caught up, pointing their guns toward the woman and boy whom they'd come to capture. Deciding it best to answer her question now, the boy started to mouth words. It wasn't out of fear that the police may kill him, but rather out of fear for what she might do to him if he didn't.

"I-I... was being chased by them."

A warning shot had been fired, yet again breaking the night's silence and the woman suddenly seemed severely agitated. She dropped the boy, turning slowly to face the officers pointing their weapons at her.

"Step away from him now!" they demanded.

She moved away without resistance, allowing the police to close in and come into contact with the one they were chasing. They had been cautious approaching him and eased by the woman, keeping a safe distance from her with guns still pointed.

"Who are you and why are you here?" they asked.

"My name is Reinia," she began in a low, eerie tone, "I live here."

The answer had irritated the police, who shifted their attention slightly more toward Reinia after hearing what could only be a blatant lie. There was no structure around here and no one would dare try making such an ominous place their abode. They challenged her, asking once more about her identity and her origin. They were sure she wasn't one of the villagers.

"No one ever visits this place. How would you know

whether I lived here or not?"

"Miss, I'll ask one more time. Who are you and what are you doing here? If you can't come clean, we'll have to take you back as well. Whether or not that's in cuffs is up to you."

The look in her eyes reflected one of anger and disappointment. She turned away from the officers and started to walk off towards the fog. One of the officers started after her, tackling her to the ground in a rough manner as he cuffed her. He hoisted her up and walked back towards the other policemen who'd also cuffed their initial target.

"I guess you'll be joining us back at the station like this," the officer said, sighing as he walked with Reinia in tow.

Her head was low. She seemed frighteningly calm for someone who'd just been tackled to the floor and acquired a few new scrapes on her skin. The officer holding her instinctively backed away despite her being confined. He began to sweat and found it hard to breathe. It felt as though he was the one captive even though she was in cuffs, and she watched as he ran off alone, ignoring shouts from his fellow officers.

"That damn idiot!" one of the other officers shouted as he rushed to grab hold of Reinia.

The police were rough, earning grunts of pain from the boy as they began making their way back into the fog. It wasn't long before their vision was once again impaired, and they felt around for the ropes outlining the trail. Everyone was becoming more tense, and the glow of Reinia's green eyes underlined their sense of unease.

"It's always the same."

Painful wails pierced the night accompanied by the sound of gunfire and the captured boy dropped to the floor in fear. The police had lost their hold on Reinia, desperately trying to regain control with deadly force after she had attacked. They fired in the direction of her eyes, but the bullets had seemed to hit nothing more than mist each time.

It was not long before both the bullets and screams subsided, and the sounds of snapping bones echoed in the boy's mind as he lay on the ground, trembling, wondering if he was next.

"What's your name?" she asked.

The boy flinched, terrified although Reinia's touch was gentle. She carried him back toward the lake as though he were a small child, and despite her earlier episode after being ignored, her gaze was soft. Whether her patience this time had been a result of her acknowledging his fear, he felt it best not to test her and stated his name through chattering teeth.

"D-Da-Damien."

Reinia took him back to the pier, dumping him into the water without any indication of her intentions. It was abrupt, and his panic coupled with a broken leg made it impossible to stay afloat. Pockets of air rose to the surface, and Damien's vision darkened, his last memory the sight of Reinia plunging into the water, dragging him deeper into its depths.

***

Damien woke to a sea-green room littered with scattered shells and sediment you'd normally find on an ocean floor. It felt as though he were being caressed by gentle waves each time he moved, making it hard to imagine actually leaving the bed. He was alive... and he felt incredible. The usual pangs of hunger and fatigue he faced during daily life were all gone, and his body seemed to be in top condition.

As he tried to get up and look around, he noticed a dresser made of what appeared to be hardened seaweed, and a mirror just above it with a coral frame. It was as if this person were obsessed with the ocean. He couldn't remember how he got here but thought it best to go thank the one who'd helped him.

Damien approached the door exiting the room whilst pondering one of its jarring designs. A curved transparent glass invited creeping darkness from the outside. It was pitch black, and the absence of any type of illuminating presence left one's imagination to run amok, thinking about lurkers of the night.

Forcing himself to ignore it, Damien opened the door only to find himself in utter shock. A girl sat nude on a couch, her head thrown back over the top delaying her notice of prying eyes. He felt as though he knew her, but his memory had failed him. She must've been asleep given how still she remained even after the noise he made upon opening the door.

Inching closer toward her, he'd realised how beautiful she was. In spite of some scars over her body, she possessed an amazing figure and pristine skin accentuated by her flowing black hair. *Was she the one who helped me? Help...ed? Where was I?* His memory was still hazy, but if he'd been in trouble, she had to be the one whom had lent him aid.

"Do you intend to stare at me all day?"

A sweet voice broke Damien's thought, and he stumbled backwards in surprise. Whilst he was lost in thought, his gaze indeed lingered upon the woman's supple breasts, but he never once thought her awake. She raised her head to see him and crossed her legs as she regarded him with piercing green eyes.

"Um... are you the one who brought me here?"

"That I am," she replied.

Damien nervously scratched his head, assiduously averting his gaze. He was uncomfortable, unable to process his own thoughts efficiently whilst in the presence of this woman in her provocative state.

There was an old dining set behind the couch that had likely seen better days. The wood had been badly chipped in numerous areas and was covered with scratches. There was a frilly blue dress draped over one of the chairs, and directly on the wall facing the couch, there was an altar made of aged, discoloured stone with luminescent green scales at the centre impaled by a bloodstained knife. It was... disconcerting.

"Nice place you've got here."

His attempt at conversation fell flat, and she scoffed, rising immediately to don the frilly blue dress she had put over the dining chair before motioning him to sit. After taking a seat on the couch she'd previously sat on, he felt a warm hand over his forehead, taking the measure of his temperature.

"You seem to be fine for now."

The girl moved to sit just across from him, both feet up in the cushions... an act that would've got most people yelled at in Damien's experience. She regarded him as if words failed her; as though her thoughts were being plucked out of her head, but she spoke.

"The name's Aeiya by the way."

"Where are we?" Damien asked quizzically, "it's incredibly dark out. Living alone like this must be terrifying."

"I've been alone out here for years. The night no longer fazes me."

"I can't say I'm comfortable in a place like this at all. It creeps me out."

"Was it well-lit where you stayed?"

"No... but I knew the area well and stayed with a friend. I know nothing of this place and frankly... the unknown scares me."

Aeiya seemed intrigued, as if she somehow wanted to test whether his statement was true. A wave of unease washed over Damien as he thought of Aeiya's curiosity about his statement and what she might try to test it.

"So let's say you knew this place... would that eliminate your fear? Because it's no longer unknown? Or would the darkness outside still cause u to be wary?"

Damien paused. "It's unlikely I'd be all right even if I knew my way around unless I'd been here for quite some time."

"Darkness then... that is your fear? Is it because that very darkness obscures what could be?"

"It's not the darkness itself per se, but unless you've

been in an area for years, you wouldn't have an idea of what're ordinary occurrences. Living alone has taught me a lot."

"Interesting. So in your eyes it all comes down to the unknown, but the unknown doesn't need to be a bad thing."

Aeiya smiled, and Damien's cheeks were visibly flushed. His previous unease was alleviated, and she kept the conversation going, sparking his interest so much that he'd completely forgotten about his actual location.

She was captivating, both in physical beauty and character. Time was lost on them during their verbal exchange, and a rising sun illuminated a scene leaving Damien bewildered. This couldn't have been the room he'd found himself in when he came to. She must've taken him to another.

The creeping darkness that sent shivers down his spine was replaced with what appeared to be the marvels of an in-house aquarium. A number of aquatic species manoeuvred around underwater plant life at incredible speed and the faint shimmer left behind by the sun's piercing rays left him in awe.

Aeiya stepped close behind him, placing her head just over his shoulder, with a satisfied look upon seeing his reaction to the outside.

"This is also the potential of the unknown."

"It'd be difficult to hope for this at all times... but I admit... it's breathtaking. An aquarium like this must cost a fortune. How'd you manage it?"

"Wait here."

Aeiya left the room with a somewhat nervous

expression, and Damien heard what he thought to be the front door open and close. His mind raced with thoughts and he wondered if she was about to show him untold riches or some type of resource that allowed her to build something like this. Whatever she was going to show him would be amazing... and it was.

Sea-green scales glistened with a gentle sheen as if kissed by moonlight, attracting a school of fish orbiting a large tail. Aeiya was a mermaid; an exceedingly stunning one at that. Her hair was decorated with miniature seashells, and was kept in a long, twisting ponytail. Shock kept Damien from fully realising he'd fallen backwards, and he watched in astonishment as she spiralled through the water in a performance worthy of a queen.

After some time had passed, she motioned him through the glass to go toward the front door and Damien quickly moved through the house so he could get a closer look at her. When he unlocked the door, rather than exit, he halted immediately.

The door led not to the outside, but into an enormous body of water that was kept at bay by some form of transparent barrier. Aeiya returned to the house, her form shifting back into that of a human's as she passed through the ward. Despite Damien's amazement at Aeiya's true nature, his mind was overwhelmed after learning it wasn't an aquarium outside.

"Aeiya..." he began, "where are we?"

"This is the bottom of lake Sym."

Silence.

The realisation that he was about three hundred feet

deep hadn't registered, leaving Damien's thoughts muddled and incoherent. The look on his face was almost despondent, as if he were contemplating giving up. He wouldn't be able to make the venture to the surface with his aquatic skills.

Aeiya moved closer to Damien, gently placing her palm against his cheek with a warm smile. He'd remained speechless, yet it seemed she understood what he was feeling.

"You aren't stuck here," she began, "I can take you back to the surface now."

Light returned to his eyes, and after short deliberation, the two agreed to resurface. The world below the lake was gorgeous, but Damien's life was on land. He couldn't stay here. Holding tightly to Aeiya, they quickly rose to the surface; her magic allowing him to breathe for the period they spent submerged.

The two came up by the pier, and Damien climbed on whilst Aeiya remained in the water. There were no signs of anyone still searching for him, and it felt like weights had just been lifted off his back. As he began to leave, he turned one last time to see his saviour.

"Thank you... Reinia."

For a moment there was a deafening silence, only to be broken thereafter by a failed attempt to retort. Damien chuckled. Reinia's stunned face was a nice parting gift, one he'd be sure to keep in memory.

"To answer your question, I remembered when you told me where we were. I wasn't sure you'd let me go given what happened up to this point... but truly... thank you."

Damien left Reinia behind as he darted off into the fog, ecstatic that he'd be able to safely return home unbothered by the authorities of Symeria. The sun was getting low now, and he'd prefer making it back before nightfall.

***

Damien came upon a cluster of trees deep within the forest, choked by an entanglement of vines. He carefully treaded between them trying to avoid being seen. Coming out on the other side of the vines, he saw the small cabin hidden behind the thicket of trees. His home.

The wooden door creaked slightly as he passed through, unveiling quaint living quarters. There was a bed made of hay and bags of stolen goods in one corner of the hut. He'd have food left for a couple weeks at best before needing to go back into town.

It felt great to finally relax; his bed a welcome comfort after a difficult time. Nightfall was on its way to greet him and Damien embraced the thought, for he was once more in an area of the known.

After resting a few hours, he decided to take a leisurely stroll under the moonlit sky. He kept his eyes peeled for signs of anyone lurking, as his mind flooded with thoughts of unfavourable outcomes if he was caught.

Paranoia. Must be.

The cool night air kissed his cheeks and Damien expertly navigated the woodland area, calming his nerves as he moved on. It wasn't long before he came upon a small river and he followed it until it filtered down a small incline into a spring.

Its waters were somewhat chilly, but a bath was overdue. As time passed with his body partly submerged, his mind became clearer. He hadn't stopped thinking of Reinia. There was just so much about her that intrigued him... yet he feared her all the same.

But she did save me...

Once he'd finished, Damien made his way back home, quickly falling into a deep slumber after lying down on his bed.

Morning broke, and Damien groggily rose to his feet. A new day meant new adventures, and after eating his fill, he ventured off into the woods scouring the forest for any valuable items he could utilise.

Days passed by and his home had become littered with tiny nuggets of gold, pieces of rope, rusty blades and an assortment of useless things like cans and string. Gazing upon his haul, Damien pondered for a moment before taking a tiny golden coin he'd found and headed for the lake.

It was already late in the evening, and no matter how many times he'd come to the lake, the fog was always unnerving. He sat at the end of the pier, sending tiny ripples through still waters with his toes. He'd hoped she was here, sitting still for a few hours to no avail.

Maybe I should try again tomorrow.

The next day brought the same result, and the day after, despite his arrival at different times each cycle. The fourth appeared to be the same, and just as he was about to return home, the water split to reveal Reinia: a beauty basking in the dim light of a crescent moon.

His eyes lit up when he saw her, and he felt relieved that he wouldn't have to go another day feeling disappointed. It felt as though she'd been avoiding him but seeing her lifted his spirit. He was happy.

"You're a strange one."

"What do you mean?" he asked.

"I hadn't expected that you'd return here. Even more than that... you kept coming back."

"So you knew I was here?"

Reinia nodded her head in response, and Damien's expression changed. He was upset. It didn't last however, as she pulled herself from the lake and sat next to him, gazing deeply into his eyes.

"What?" he asked.

Pulling slightly away from the deadlock of their eyes, she spoke. "I was sure that you wouldn't return after what I'd done to you. I thought maybe you only came back to hurt me."

She felt vulnerable, in ways that seemed odd to Damien eliciting a moderate chuckle.

"What's so funny?" she asked slightly bothered.

"You thinking that I could hurt you when I'm positive I couldn't even if I tried. I found myself thinking of you... that's why I came back."

"Why would you be thinking of me?"

Damien fidgeted with the coin he'd brought, avoiding eye contact with Reinia, aware that she hadn't taken her gaze off him after his previous statement.

"I... I guess... I'm attracted to you."

Reinia cocked her head in amusement, bewildered

upon hearing Damien's confession. She'd lived here for a few lifetimes, and humans always threatened her life, yet this one claimed to be into her? Unheard of.

"You really are a weird one."

Reinia moved closer to Damien, notably ruffling his feathers and she smiled. His discomfort was cute, and the two spent a large portion of the night deep in conversation. It was free flowing... unforced and intriguing.

"I got you something."

Damien handed Reinia the coin he'd found some days ago, unsure of how she'd react. It wasn't of any real use as money as it differed from local currency but to a collector it was a rare find. None of it mattered however, as he'd just wanted her to have something of his.

Reinia's cheeks were flushed, and Damien felt ecstatic. He wanted badly to spend more time with her... and he would.

"Do you want to come see where I stay tomorrow?"

Reinia's face darkened, and her voice was solemn as she spoke.

"I was bound to this lake a few centuries ago by the founders of Symeria. I'm not able to wander very far from here."

Damien unexpectedly hugged Reinia, and instead of making a fuss, he'd assured her that he'd be back to see her daily. Her smile felt much more satisfying now, and she walked with him up to the edge of the fog.

"I'll have to part ways here. Get home safely Damien."

The two hugged once more before leaving, anxiously

awaiting the coming days with large grins upon their faces.

The next few months had deepened their connection, and the two grew inseparable. Days Damien needed to procure food worried Reinia, as he'd sometimes come close to being caught by the authorities and she could do naught but await his return.

She'd spoil him by taking him deep underwater, marvelling at the aquatic scenery as he freely swam within the lake's depths and he would do small things for her such as leaving trails to midnight dinners or making mementos for her to cherish. Her favourite was a chain made of tightened string which held the very first gift he'd given her.

Reinia held the coin tightly against her chest as this night was no different. She awaited his return from the occasional food excursion, and her chest tightened as the hours passed by. She didn't want to lose him… to return to a life of solitude after her heart had been opened, but Damien never came.

Two days passed.

Venturing to the edge of the fog, Reinia forced herself from its veil and immediately felt weakened. The lake's waters became chaotic, and a low rumble resonated through the forest to the village. Each step she took saw ever so slight increases in the magnitude of the tremors as well as faster siphons of her life force.

She struggled to reach the village's gates, and Reinia fell to her knees with a blank stare. Damien's luck had run out, and the village had left him crucified at the entrance. Tears fell from lifeless eyes, and Reinia felt a well of emotion build inside her as she took in the sight of the man she loved, left for the crows.

One of the villagers had passed by and spat at the ground beneath Damien's feet before attempting to help Reinia.

This had to be a sick joke.

The touch of this cretin made Reinia boil with rage, and despite her fading life, she forced her body to withstand her magic for just a few minutes more. The maggot's crushed throat prevented it from screaming, and an immensely thick fog creeped in on the small village.

A fading life meant nothing against the turmoil she'd been experiencing, and Reinia snuffed the life out of every living creature she could find in a brutal massacre. The haunting cries of the villagers and their children, the animals, all gave Reinia a feeling of satisfaction.

What followed was a hollow silence, and she removed Damien's body, placing him on the grass just a few feet away from the city gates. She hadn't the strength left to go any further, and she lay next to him, clasping the coin between their palms as droplets of rain embraced their cold bodies.

Reinia's life faded in an area she detested, comforted only by the touch of the man she loved.

Mount Asvien

Wintry winds kissed the face of a bloodied, lonesome man as he trudged on through deep mounds of snow, unsure of if he'd reach his destination. The mountain was treacherous, and some of his team had slipped on patches of ice beneath the snow, only to fall to their demise or find their bodies braced against the jagged formations of rock not yet coated by frost.

His arms were torn, and several gashes over his body had been wrapped with pieces of cloth from his clothes, making other areas more susceptible to the sting of frigid air. There was an opening at the mountain's summit, likely a cavern, and though he was close, his sluggish movement made it a painful journey.

Mount Asvien was shrouded in myth; untold legends passed down for generations that remained unsolved. No one who'd climbed the mountain ever returned, piquing Sheran's curiosity, which was what had led to his current expedition. He'd come to regret it, fighting a losing battle in an unforgiving environment alone with an almost broken will.

The team he'd brought with him now lay inches beneath the snow, covered in pure, white flakes masking the horrors of the mountain. It was gorgeous to look at, in all its glory surrounded by thick woods that seemed to bow before its majesty.

Baffled by the inexplicable deaths of his crew, Sheran's movements were somewhat erratic as he constantly panicked with each passing step. Fear kept him at the mercy of the elements for an extended period as he constantly wondered if each new step may lead to a slip and eventually his death.

As he drew closer to the mountain's peak and to safety, thick pockets of snow periodically blew by, obscuring his vision while heightened winds threatened to throw him off balance. Covering a distance as small as fifty feet took him another ten minutes, and by the time he'd made it into the cavern, his body shivered uncontrollably.

Sheran longed for warmth, forcing him deeper into the cavern depths and away from chilling winds at the entrance. Using the rugged cavern walls for support, he made his way into the dark abyss, hopeful that another person lived inside after witnessing etched drawings of what he thought to be an indigenous tribe dancing around an open flame.

It wasn't long before he was unable to perceive anything but darkness, and each step he'd made was calculated. The walls he clung to and the coarse floor beneath were his guide in an opaque hollow he knew nothing of.

Winding through tight pathways, the whistling winds which brought the sting of winter became naught but a distant echo. He found himself crawling through a small opening in the walls, fighting back grunts of pain due to his wounds as he pushed forward to investigate the faint noise from liquid splattering against the cavern floor.

Sheran carefully creeped out of the small tunnel, firmly holding rocky protrusions above so he could safely feel for the floor beneath. He wouldn't forfeit his life by assuming the path didn't lead to an open chasm.

It wasn't.

The moment his feet touched the floor a gentle breeze kissed his body, drowning his worries with a surreal feeling of serenity. The space he'd entered somehow became illuminated, as if the crystals above were cued by his arrival. An odd shimmer piqued his interest, plastering the room in a boggling array of colour.

A grass trail led up to a hut in the centre of the room surrounded by a moat, and on either side was a mechanism filtering a black liquid into it. Directly behind the hut on the other side of the room were two massive, white stone doors with a symbol resembling a closed fist. The door was guarded by two rugged earthen statues firmly clasping stone tablets too difficult to read from such a distance.

"Hello?" Sheran called out.

He awaited a reply that never came, and once sure he was alone, Sheran followed the path to the hut, meticulously avoiding any of the black liquid from the moat. The door creaked open under a slight touch, and the sweet scent of magnolia blossoms graced his nose. A dusty wooden cabinet with its doors tied shut by a dark red rosary was the first thing Sheran noticed amongst the clutter.

There was a small round table in the centre of the hut and a plate made of the crystals outside harboured an unfinished chicken leg coated by a thin layer of dust. A bag just underneath held hiking gear which Sheran inspected to determine whether he could make the trip back down once he was ready to leave. Water pails, brushes, and a bucket of red paint toppled over next to a large mound of hay decorated the other side of the room but were of no consequence to Sheran.

He was weary, and the almost hidden markings on the round table interested him more than the unkempt state of the room. He wiped as much dust away as possible, revealing hieroglyphic text that left him slightly confused.

Fallen are the held. Life abound to he who is free.

Did he need to leave? The true meaning behind the words engraved on the table eluded him, but his body was also unable to withstand a trip back down the mountain in his current state. Leaving the area would have to wait until he recovered. In order to rest, Sheran left the hut through the door he'd entered, closing it behind him to minimise the amount of dust that escaped. The earthen floor was less than comfy, but it would suffice given the absence of threatening cold winds this far in the cave.

Unaware of how much time had passed, Sheran woke from a deep slumber. His body ached, and the wounds he'd sustained had progressively gotten worse while he slept. Leaving felt more like a fleeting dream as time moved on, and even as he ransacked the entire hut hoping to find some type of medicinal ointment, his efforts were in vain.

The only place left to check was the cabinet barred shut by the rosary which upon opening revealed an old diary, parchment and writing instruments. The diary's cover was brittle to the touch and Sheran carefully handled it to reduce the possibility of obscuring the contents.

Someone had made it here before him.

Like himself, this person had come seeking to unveil the mysteries of the mount and was gravely injured in the process. Assuming their word was true, bathing in the tar-like liquid of the moat would cure his wounds. They had spent an inordinate amount of time within the cave investigating its contents as well as trying to decipher the meaning of the messages left behind.

The diary trailed off after details stating that the person had ventured beyond the towering stone doors behind the hut. None of that was of any immediate consequence however, as Sheran needed to be free of his ailments. The thought of submerging himself within the black liquid seemed insane, but he was stripped of a choice. He would soon succumb to his wounds without treatment and no other options were available to him.

Sheran left the hut and stood at the edge of the moat, staring into the dark concoction he had to subject himself to with uncertainty. Forcing himself to move, Sheran closed his eyes as he fell inside. Weakness left his body, and he was somehow able to breathe despite his entire body being engulfed by a foreign liquid. He needn't panic, and once all his wounds had been healed, he resurfaced, climbing back onto the pathway.

His excitement couldn't be contained, and he wondered what other treasures the mount held if a pool of such advanced medicinal properties lay in such an accessible area. The discoveries he'd make if he ventured beyond the door could be monumental, and it meant his team... his friends... they wouldn't have perished for naught.

Standing at the base of the stone doors, Sheran's face furrowed with a quizzical look. The text inscribed on the tablet held by the statue to the left was incomprehensible, and he wasn't sure what to make of it. It read:

Ask of us all
Sacrifice beyond must
Held in the fall

The tablet held by the adjacent statue offered less illusion, detailing how to open the stone doors and enter.

Bathe and clear your mind
Match the symbol and enter

Sheran was positive his submergence in the black liquid was his bath, and matching the symbol meant to touch the doors with his fist. Nothing could go wrong... right? There was a low rumble once Sheran touched the symbol, and the doors slowly opened inward.

He stepped into a long corridor, lit by overhead crystals as the last room was. The pathway twisted and turned, leading down into the depths of the mountain. It took Sheran another twenty minutes before he'd come upon another white door, only this one was made of metal and was of a normal size. Placing his fist on the symbol in the centre of it served to unlock this barrier as well, and he came into a quaint space.

Artefacts made of gold piled high in one corner of the room, and three mounds of dirt lay at the base. Likely graves. Sheran made up his mind to check what lie beneath, but the etchings on the wall drew his attention.

An individual was bound, escorted into a chamber after passing through two others and made to kneel before a council. Whilst here, the stitches binding their mouth shut came undone, and the council revered the captive once they'd spoken. Scratching his head, Sheran chuckled to himself. This scenario would be foolish to think about in the real world as a captive.

Moving over to the artefacts, he came to the realisation that it'd be impossible to leave the mount carrying many of them and sighed to himself. It meant carefully choosing which he'd depart with, as he had no intention of returning to the treacherous mount once home. The fame and prestige he'd accumulate just from being the one who discovered the place would be enough.

After sifting through the pile, he'd settled on a crystal dagger with a golden hilt, a chalice decorated with rare gems and a gorgeous black blade with a thin, linked chain on its hilt. Skeletons lay beneath the dirt mounds, each simply wearing a chain bearing a letter pendant. The first was the letter K, while the other two had pendants S and A. The chains probably meant a lot to them while they were alive and given that they'd been buried with them, Sheran thought it best to leave their treasured belongings in the grave. Covering the graves again took some time, and once he'd finished, he moved on to exit the room through yet another white door, only carrying the dagger to minimise weight as he explored.

He found himself descending through a pathway yet another twenty minutes before reaching the next entrance, and once inside, he found another etching on the walls. A member of the council left with the previous captive, and once reaching the door holding the symbol, the council member pierced their own heart with a dagger, sending the captive into a rage.

There was an altar within the room with an empty clamp above it. It fit the dagger he'd brought perfectly, but Sheran wasn't about to leave his only weapon behind. Just below the altar were a few totems, cracked and worn. It was clear the people who lived here had some type of religious practice... but whom did they worship?

If he wanted answers he'd need to travel even deeper into the mountain, and so he did. The final path stretched for forty minutes, and there was no door blocking the entrance to the last room. It was bigger than the previous two, and a black pool off to the side piqued his interest. There were special containers by its edge, as if beckoning newcomers to leave with the special healing concoction.

Sheran noticed a woman dark of complexion asleep with her back against the wall on the side farthest from the pool with bandaged arms. Could she be the one responsible for the diary back in the hut? Sheran had so many questions, but he decided to go after viewing the markings on the wall.

The markings detailed the captive submerging themself within the pool, emerging with a powerful glow that cast a large shadow. He was alone in this area and began his ascent out of the mount after his revitalisation. There was an inscription at the end, and Sheran's eyes shone at the translation. *Life eternal to those who rise from the depths.*

Stifling his urge to dive in the bay was difficult, but he needed to confirm whether the girl was alive. Sheran crossed over to her lying position and placed his hand on her shoulder, causing her to immediately wake up and back away in a panic.

"Calm down," Sheran began, "I'm not here to hurt you."

His voice was quiet, soothing. He made no sudden movement, allowing the girl to steel her nerves more quickly. She still moved away, refusing to show her back to someone she'd never seen.

"I'm Sheran. I came here on an expedition to discover the secrets of this place. Are you the one who wrote that diary in the hut?"

Silence. The girl seemed to be processing what he'd said and slapped herself as if to be sure she wasn't hallucinating. Regarding him with curious eyes she began to speak in a raspy tone.

"Never… expected to see someone here…"

She sounded parched, as if she hadn't a drop to drink for a long time, and each word felt forced as they left her lips.

"How long have you been here?" Sheran asked.

"The diary you spoke of… I wrote it one hundred years ago."

One hundred years? She must've said it in jest. This woman hadn't looked a day over thirty, yet those soft, hazel eyes showed no sign of deceit.

"How's that possible?" he asked.

She nodded towards the black pool as if to say it gave her everlasting life. The inscription was true? Then the markings on the walls… maybe each provided some clue to other secrets he'd not yet found. He was unable to hide his elation, and his smile somewhat unnerved his companion.

As Sheran continued to ask about the mountain, he noticed that what he originally thought were tiny marks or freckles around her lips were small incisions. He paused, pondering the reason someone's mouth might've been pierced the way hers was and pieces of a puzzle he had no clue how to solve came together.

"What is it?" she asked.

The change in his gaze was noticed by the girl, and he awkwardly chuckled, apologising while lost in thought. The etchings in the first room detailed a captive with their mouth sewn shut, and if she represented that captive, then he needed to question her. He was in the final chamber, which explained the loss of whatever sealed her lips.

"Why are you here?"

"I was trapped," she replied, "The day I was granted eternal life was also the day I lost my freedom. If you choose to submerge yourself, the doors slowly begin to close, and they cannot be opened from this side. My mistake was trying to bottle the liquid to take with me. My desire for money and fame kept me here longer and I lost my chance to leave."

Her greed explained the containers by the pool's edge, but he needed to know more.

"Was there anyone else here when you came?"

"I was alone throughout my time here. I sometimes spoke to the three graves in the first chamber. It's where I slept my first few days here, and I woke to find my lips sewn on the third. Only after I reached this chamber and stepped into the pool was I able to speak again."

"What about the middle chamber? Were you able to figure it out?"

"The people here worshipped some deity, but I'm not sure what. My assumption was that without sacrifice the mountain would be treacherous, but we managed to make it here... I think we could make it back down given my newfound immortality."

Sheran listened closely to all she had to say, and their conversation continued for a time yet, until he decided to acquire immortality himself. There would be no need for him to offer sacrifice once he'd obtained it, and he couldn't think of another reason that the mount's weather was so volatile. Her thoughts coincided with his own about the etchings and what he thought of the place, so they both decided to run headlong for the exit once he'd dipped in the liquid.

The two made it to the centre chamber as the doors had been closed halfway and they ran flat out towards the first, ignoring a trembling altar as they passed through. It wasn't long before they reached the first chamber, and Sheran, risking entrapment, picked up the sword and chalice he'd set aside, inching through a slim gap as the door closed behind him.

The two of them were out of breath, and Sheran smiled, ecstatic that they'd made it out and made such a discovery. He tried to open the doors once more, and though he was on the side they'd originally opened from, the doors remained shut.

"We're not allowed to enter again I suppose."

"I suppose not. I have to ask though..." she said as

she placed her hand on his shoulder, "were you ever able to figure out the riddle behind this tablet?"

She'd been referring to the one he'd initially found incomprehensible, and Sheran's face remained puzzled.

"I couldn't make sense of it to be honest. Rearranging the words doesn't help either."

"That's because you weren't supposed to." Her voice started to change. "Not everything you see here is important. This girl figured it out."

This girl.

Sheran tried to pull away but despite their being no real grip, he was unable to move, forced to watch a shadowy figure unfurl in place of the dark girl who had been speaking to him. Sweat trickled down his cheeks, and terror set in his eyes. The shadow seeped into him through his pores, and Sheran lost all control of his body. He was a passenger, one who could hear the shadow speak to him whilst his body made its way back through the cave.

It took her days to realise, but she figured out that the etchings were not entirely true. Had you pondered a bit more maybe you would've too. She even managed to leave a clue to help the next traveller if they were unlucky enough to make it here. KSA... did you not think the pendants on those chains had meaning? The tablet utilised keywords and diversions. Ask... Sacrifice... Held. Those pendants she'd left behind were for you, the next person, to realise that was the correct room to ask your questions. I cannot lie or manipulate while in that chamber. I've been bound to this place for generations, unable to leave unless someone refused to make a sacrifice while held. The last etching was a warning; the shadow cast by those emerging from the pool signifying my hold on your soul, but many would readily jump to immortality without a second thought. You made your choices based on desire without thought, Sheran, and now... all must fall.

Sheran made it back to the cavern entrance, breathing frigid air for the first time. Neither terrain nor weather seemed to bother him, and he took his first steps down the mountain. A brief clearing of the clouds above offered a glimpse at shadowy pockets of darkness where his eyes should be and a taunting smirk.

Now I am free.

www.ingramcontent.com/pod-product-compliance
Ingram Content Group UK Ltd.
Pitfield, Milton Keynes, MK11 3LW, UK
UKHW041946230426
12048UKWH00008B/162